THE UNDERWEAR WOLF

'The Underwear Wolf'

An original concept by Clare Helen Welsh

Illustrated by Letizia Rizzo

Published by MAVERICK ARTS PUBLISHING LTD

Studio 3A, City Business Centre, 6 Brighton Road,

Horsham, West Sussex, RH13 5BB

+44 (0)1403 256941

A CIP catalogue record for this book is available at the British Library.

ISBN 978-1-84886-397-2

www.maverickbooks.co.uk

Gold

This book is rated as: Gold Band (Guided Reading)

THE UNDERWEAR WOLF

By Clare Helen Welsh

Illustrated by
Letizia Rizzo

Chapter 1

Right from the beginning Stitch knew he was different. He had two eyes like the other children. He had a nose and hair on his head like the other children, too.

But Stitch had a secret. When the full moon shone in the night sky, his feet became furry. Hairs sprouted all over his hands. His voice grew deep and growly. Because Stitch... was a werewolf.

On a full moon, Stitch wasn't tucked up in bed reading a story like the other children. He was outside, exploring!

On a full moon, Stitch wasn't sound asleep dreaming of bouncy castles and fluffy rabbit tails. He was racing through the forest chasing beetles and fireflies!

Even in the day light, Stitch stood out. He tried going to school once...

...but he didn't really fit in.

So Stitch spent his days all by himself. He loved knitting and stitching. He designed the most marvellous scarves. He darned the most fabulous socks. He knitted the most spectacular jumpers.

But there's only so many knitted scarves and jumpers

one werewolf can wear. Stitch often dreamed of a friend to race and chase and knit for. And then one moonlit night...

"Awroooooooooo!"

...he heard one!

Chapter 2

Stitch couldn't believe his luck! He raced through the forest as fast as his furry legs could carry him.

It wasn't long before he found exactly what he was looking for. But Stitch didn't just find one werewolf...

...he found a whole pack!

"Hi! I'm Stitch! It's nice to meet you!" he said.

But his new friends weren't so sure.

"Why are you wearing clothes?" they giggled.

"You're supposed to take them off!" they chuckled.

"How cute! He made them himself!" they laughed.

It seemed Stitch had a lot to learn about being a werewolf.

"Do you know how to prowl?" the werewolves asked.

"Do you know how to howl?" they asked again.

"Have you ever been part of a pack before?" they said.

Stitch had to admit. He didn't and he hadn't.

"You're pretty weird for a werewolf!" the pack sniggered. And in a flash of fur and bushy tails, they ran off together into the forest.

A lonely tear rolled down Stitch's cheek.

He trudged back to his den all on his own.

He was so upset, he didn't even notice the pack coming back for him.

"Aren't you coming?" the werewolves asked. "We never leave a wolf behind, even if they are a bit embarrassing!"

Chapter 3

Stitch spent the month learning everything he needed to know for the next full moon. He had daily prowling practice.

"Got ya!"

He had evening howling lessons.

"Yap! Yap!"

He learned lots of new things.

But the other werewolves still weren't sure about him. They teased him a bit too.

Stitch didn't mind though, because knitting made him happy. In his spare time, he snipped and stitched and knitted just as before.

And when the next full moon rose high in the night's sky, Stitch was careful to remember everything he had learned.

He met the other werewolves in the special clearing in the forest.

“Hello everyone! Sorry I’m late!” he called.

And this time he was wearing nothing whatsoever...

...nothing except some super stretchy knitted underwear!

Chapter 4

“What kind of werewolf wears patterned pants?” the werewolves teased.

Stitch looked around. He was the odd one out again. All of the other werewolves had

already taken their clothes off and put them into neat, little piles, being careful to tuck their socks into their shoes.

“And why didn’t your underwear tear when you transformed?” they puzzled. Stitch told them all about his special stretchy wool, and then insisted on keeping his underwear on.

‘Who knows where we could end up?’ he thought.

Under the silver, starlit sky, the werewolves raced through the forest.

Stitch kept up all the way. And when they played hide and seek... he found them all in record time!

“It’s those stretchy pants! They’re giving me the giggles!” said one werewolf to another.

The werewolves were having so much fun, they didn’t even notice the first rays of daylight rising on the horizon.

Bright beams of sunshine trickled through the leafy forest, and at that very moment...

...the pack began to change!

The fur on their feet disappeared.

The hair on their hands vanished.

Their voices were no longer deep and growling but sweet and childlike.

Of course, there was a very big problem.

They had no idea where they were and, without their werewolf senses, they couldn't find their clothes anywhere!

Chapter 5

"Oh no! Not *again!*" the werewolves wailed.

This time Stitch didn't mind being the odd one out. Instead, he felt *rather* smug. Chilly, but smug!

"You just never know where you're going to end up!" he smiled.

Suddenly his super stretchy knitted pants

didn’t seem like such a bad idea.

Maybe… just maybe… all the werewolves needed a pair.

That month, Stitch snipped, stitched and knitted more than ever before.

And the next time the silvery, round moon appeared in high the sky... the pack was prepared!

“Hip, hip hooray for Stitch!” they cheered.

Stitch had to admit, they were his wildest designs yet!

The underwear werewolves celebrated with a party. They danced in the undergrowth and sang amongst the fireflies. They told anyone who would listen about Stitch and his stretchy pants.

Stitch was so happy, he danced and sang and then...

...he howled!

"You can howl!" the pack cheered and everyone smiled, but Stitch's smile was the biggest.

Finally he was part of a pack who loved him.
And he loved them too.

Maybe even more than knitting!

The End

Pink
Red
Yellow
Blue
Green
Orange
Turquoise
Purple
Gold
White

Book Bands for Guided Reading

The Institute of Education book banding system is a scale of colours that reflects the various levels of reading difficulty. The bands are assigned by taking into account the content, the language style, the layout and phonics. Word, phrase and sentence level work is also taken into consideration.

Maverick Early Readers are a bright, attractive range of books covering the pink to white bands. All of these books have been book banded for guided reading to the industry standard and edited by a leading educational consultant.

To view the whole Maverick Readers scheme, visit our website at www.maverickearlyreaders.com

Or scan the QR code above to view our scheme instantly!